MARTIAL ARTS

AND THEIR GREATEST FIGHTERS

inside sports

MARTIAL ARTS
AND THEIR GREATEST FIGHTERS

EDITED BY MARTY GITLIN

Britannica®
Educational Publishing
IN ASSOCIATION WITH

ROSEN
EDUCATIONAL SERVICES

Published in 2015 by Britannica Educational Publishing (a trademark of Encyclopædia Britannica, Inc.) in association with The Rosen Publishing Group, Inc.
29 East 21st Street, New York, NY 10010

Distributed exclusively by Rosen Publishing.
To see additional Britannica Educational Publishing titles, go to rosenpublishing.com.

First Edition

Britannica Educational Publishing
J. E. Luebering: Director, Core Reference Group
Anthony L. Green: Editor, Compton's by Britannica

Rosen Publishing
Hope Lourie Killcoyne: Executive Editor
Nelson Sá: Art Director
Michael Moy: Designer
Cindy Reiman: Photography Manager
Introduction and supplementary material by Marty Gitlin.

Library of Congress Cataloging-in-Publication Data

Martial arts and their greatest fighters / edited by Marty Gitlin. — First edition.
        pages cm. — (Inside sports)
Includes bibliographical references and index.
ISBN 978-1-62275-588-2 (library bound)
1. Martial arts — Juvenile literature. 2. Martial artists — Juvenile literature. I. Gitlin, Marty, editor of compilation.
GV1101.35.M37 2015
796.8 — dc23
                                                            2014024022

Manufactured in the United States of America

On the cover, page 3: Fighters Terrion Ware (L) and Eric Winston. *Chelsea Lauren/Getty Images for BAMMA USA*

Pages 6–7, 11, 30, 44, 56, 69, 70, 72, 76, 78 © iStockphoto.com/LSOphoto; pp. 14, 18, 38, 39, 40 Neil Lockhart/Shutterstock.com; back cover, interior pages background image nobeastsofierce/ Shutterstock.com; silhouettes Amitofo/Shutterstock.com.

CONTENTS

INTRODUCTION

Martial arts are any of a variety of fighting sports or skills. They are most often associated with combat between individuals, but they are also practiced to promote self-defense and fitness. Many people around the world use martial arts to improve their physical, emotional, spiritual, and mental health.

Martial arts can be traced to ancient cultures. Paintings on Egyptian pyramids dating as far back as 3400 BCE depict battles that can be linked to martial arts. Poems and other forms of writing around that time also describe early forms of combat that can be associated with martial arts. Drawings in Vietnam about 500 years later show that primitive armed martial arts had been practiced in Asia. These drawings display the use of spears, bows, and swords.

More modern martial arts extend back to means of combat in sixteenth-century Europe. The term was first used to describe fencing as

Buddhist monks practice kung fu at Shaolin Monastery on Mount Song in China. The Shaolin monks are renowned for their prowess in the martial arts. **Nancy Brown/Photolibrary/Getty Images**

far back as 1639. But such disciplines as kung fu, judo, karate, and kendo are mostly linked to East Asia.

Martial arts can be divided into the unarmed and armed styles of battle and sport. The origins of European martial arts included the use of archery and spears. Those styles were practiced later in Japan. Unarmed martial arts were born and developed in China. They stressed striking with feet or hands. The advancement of martial arts in Asia also

Two students practice kendo drills using shinai, *wooden (usually bamboo) swords. Kendo, the Japanese style of fencing, originated from the fighting methods of the ancient warrior class, called the samurai.* **Boston Globe/Getty Images**

included the use of everyday work tools such as sickles and knives.

In modern times, offshoots of some of the armed martial arts, such as kendo (fencing) and kyudo (archery), are practiced as sports. Spinoffs of unarmed forms of battle such as judo, sumo wrestling, karate, and tae kwon do are also embraced. So are self-defense forms, such as aikido, hapkido, and kung fu.

Forms of martial arts once used in fighting, including a Chinese style of unarmed combat called tai chi chuan, have also been simplified for peaceful purposes. They have been used to improve health and spiritual well-being.

East Asian martial arts boast a strong tie to mental and spiritual strength. That sets them apart from martial arts disciplines practiced elsewhere. East Asian martial arts are heavily influenced by religions of the region such as Taoism and Zen Buddhism. They place an emphasis on creating an ideal relationship between body and mind so the two can work in unison. The goal is to shut down the calculating and rationalizing functions of the mind. That shutdown allows the mind to react immediately and in harmony with the body to whatever situation it might encounter.

This book will examine some of the martial arts forms from their beginnings in Asia

to their growing influence around the world at the present time. It will also introduce readers to historic figures whose martial arts have long been celebrated. Today's martial arts stars who stand out for their exceptional fighting techniques are also profiled, exemplifying the rich culture of the martial arts that continues to capture the interest of athletes who want to master the variety of attack and defense skills the sports offer. These noteworthy figures have contributed greatly to the evolution of martial arts as a legitimate and highly regulated form of athletics and competition.

CHAPTER 1

AN OVERVIEW OF MARTIAL ARTS

T he term *martial arts* refers to a large variety of fighting sports originating in Europe and East Asia, but practiced in modern times around the world. The word "martial" is derived from Mars, the Roman god of war. It is used to describe activities with a combative bent. Many of the martial arts, however, are not combative. Some are meditative forms of self-discipline with strong religious or philosophical overtones. They are heavily influenced by Eastern religion and emphasize mental and spiritual training.

Folktales and mythologies cloud the origins of martial arts.

Buddhist monks fight bare handed before Chinese dignitaries. Herve BRUHAT/ Gamma-Rapho/Getty Images

One popular legend holds that Buddhist monks in China developed kung fu around 500 CE after learning the skill from Indian monk and Zen Buddhism founder Bodhidharma. Fighting systems were developed in Asia thousands of years ago by military organizations and secret societies. Most of the East Asian systems were heavily influenced by ancient practices that originated in India and China.

MARTIAL ARTS IN CHINA

Although many in the West think of Chinese martial arts as kung fu, that phrase simply means "skill." It can be used to describe a talent for painting, cooking, or any other activity. In modern China *wushu* is the term used to cover all the martial arts. Wushu originated in China at least 2,500 years ago. There are hundreds of styles.

Eastern religions have had strong influences on wushu. Wushu can be a combination of combat techniques. It may be practiced as exercise or as a performing art.

The varieties of wushu are typically considered either external or internal. The external arts are known for their powerful kicks and punches and speedy movements. Internal arts tend to be less combative and oriented toward self-defense.

Some forms of wushu take their inspiration from animals, such as the monkey or eagle, and attempt to imitate their fighting styles. Many forms allow for the use of weapons, such as swords or staffs.

Kung Fu

Kung fu is a spiritual form of exercise requiring concentration and self-discipline. It is a mostly unarmed mode of personal combat often tied to karate or tae kwon do. The term *kung fu* can also suggest careful preparation for the performance of any skill performed instinctively without thought process or emotion.

Kung fu can be traced as a martial art to the Zhou dynasty (1111–255 BCE) and even earlier. The various movements in kung fu mostly imitate the fighting styles of animals. They feature one of five basic foot positions: normal upright posture and the four stances called dragon, frog, horse riding, and snake. There are hundreds of styles of kung fu. Armed and unarmed techniques have been developed.

YIN AND YANG

The terms *yin* and *yang* originated in ancient Chinese philosophy. Yin and yang mean literally the "dark side" and the "sunny side" of a hill. In Chinese and much other Eastern thought, they represent the opposites of which the world is thought to be composed: dark and light, female and male, Earth and heaven, death and birth, matter and spirit. Each makes up for what the other lacks. The wholeness of the world would be incomplete if one was lacking.

Together the yin and yang are depicted as a circle, one half dark and the other half light (this symbol appears on the flag of South Korea). Within the dark half there is a small light circle, and within the light half there is a small dark one. This suggests that, though opposites, there is a needed relationship between the two. Neither exists in and of itself alone.

TAI CHI CHUAN

Tai chi chuan is also called tai chi, or Chinese boxing. It is drawn from the principles of *taiji*. Taiji brings yin and yang together in harmony—yin as the passive principle and yang as the active principle. Tai chi chuan

A Taoist monk (wearing white) on Mount Wudang, in China's Hubei Province, leads exercises in tai chi chuan. **Karl Johaentges/LOOK/ Getty Images**

is considered a martial art and may be used with or without weapons.

Exercise to promote health was practiced in China as early as the 3rd century. By the 5th century, monks at the Buddhist monastery of Shaolin were performing exercises imitating the five creatures: bear, bird, deer, monkey, and tiger. By the early Ming dynasty (beginning in 1368), the yin and yang principles had

been added to provide harmony to the exercise activity.

The number of exercise forms in tai chi chuan vary from 24 to 108 or more. The forms are named for the image created when executed, such as "Fall back and twist like monkey." All start from one of three stances: weight forward, weight on rear foot, and legs spread as if riding a horse.

China is not the only nation in that region with a rich martial arts history tied to religion. Japan also boasts the same tradition of martial arts as a means of exercise and competition, as well as mental and emotional strength.

MARTIAL ARTS IN JAPAN

Many of the best-known martial arts in Japan arose from the practices of the famous samurai warriors, who were strongly influenced by Zen Buddhism. One goal of Zen is a state of individual insight and an emotional escape from the world. Japanese samurai found in Zen a means of improving their combat readiness and skill. Samurai who embraced Zen rid themselves of fear, even in regard to pain and the threat of death.

The building, or dojo, in which a samurai learned his arts was originally part of a

Buddhist temple. The martial arts teacher, or sensei, was the master of his dojo, and his position often was handed down by older family members. Today martial arts are more important as competitive sports and as aids to physical and mental fitness.

Martial arts such as jujitsu (or jujutsu), kenjutsu, and ninjutsu are mostly combative. Others emphasize *do*, which is how the Japanese pronounce the Chinese word *dao* and means the "way of enlightenment." Meditation and highly skillful methods of self-defense are part of their training. Among these are aikido, kendo, and judo.

JUJITSU

Japanese *jujitsu* (meaning "gentle art") is not so gentle at all. It is a method of fighting that makes use of few or no weapons, but it features holds, throws, and blows to subdue an opponent.

Jujitsu evolved among the warrior class (the samurai) in Japan from about the 17th century. Designed to heighten a warrior's fencing skills in combat, it was a ruthless style. Its usual object of warfare was crippling or killing an attacker. It involves techniques of hitting, kicking, kneeing,

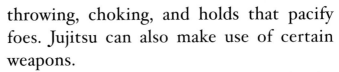

throwing, choking, and holds that pacify foes. Jujitsu can also make use of certain weapons.

These systems revolve around the concept *ju*, from a Chinese character commonly interpreted as "gentle." In this case, "gentle" means giving way to an opponent's direction of attack while attempting to control it. Also involved was the use of hard or tough parts of the body such as knuckles, fists, elbows, and knees against an enemy's weakest points.

Jujitsu declined in the late 19th century, but has enjoyed renewed popularity since the 1990s.

THE SAMURAI WARRIOR

Samurai warriors were not only martial arts experts in Japan from the 12th to 19th centuries. They also led the government. They wielded almost complete power over the country.

The first samurai protected the estates of those in the upper class. They later remained in the capital to serve in military needs and put down rebellions, though they continued to safeguard the property of the nobility. They grew so powerful that by 1185 a samurai gained total military control of the nation. He claimed the title of "shogun" as the samurai became the ruling class in Japan. Shoguns continued to rule the nation for 700 years.

Samurai warriors during this period held themselves to a strict code of conduct called Bushido, which means "way of the warrior." The code held to a high standard such attributes as bravery, honor, loyalty, and discipline. Those ideals proved to be more important than life itself. In fact, samurai that lost a battle or allowed those he was protecting to be killed often committed suicide because he had not fulfilled his duty.

Changes in Japanese society eventually weakened the role of the samurai warrior. Lower-ranking samurai grew eager to create a stronger nation

A samurai wears a helmet decorated with animal horns, perhaps to scare an opponent. **Library of Congress, Washington, D.C.**

as Western powers set sights on gaining influence in the country. Many samurai become involved in a movement that overthrew the shogun leadership in 1868. The new government, led by the emperor Meiji, stripped the samurai of their power. It also put down samurai rebellions launched to regain their status.

AIKIDO

Aikido, which in English means "way of harmonizing energy," is a martial art and self-defense system. It resembles the fighting methods jujitsu and judo in its use of twisting and throwing techniques. Aikido fighters train to subdue, rather than injure or kill. But many of their movements can be deadly anyway. Aikido stresses the importance of calmness and body control to overcome the attack of an opponent.

The basic skills of aikido probably originated in Japan in about the 14th century. In the early 20th century they were structured in their modern form through the work of Japanese martial arts expert Ueshiba Morihei.

There are no offensive moves in aikido. As taught by Ueshiba, it was so purely defensive an art that no direct contest between practitioners was possible. His student Tomiki Kenji developed a competition style (known as Tomiki aikido) that merged aikido techniques. A competitor attempts to score points by swiftly touching an opponent with a rubber or wooden knife and the other tries to avoid and disarm the attacker. The two take turns wielding the knife.

Aikido self-defense techniques include wrist-lock moves and throws, which turn the attacker from a position of strength to one of surrender. **Aping Vision/STS/Photodisc/Getty Images**

JUDO

Judo was originally a Japanese system of unarmed combat, but now it is primarily a sport. Its rules are complex; the objective is to cleanly throw, pin, or master a foe. The latter is achieved by applying pressure to arm joints or to the neck to cause the opponent to surrender.

A woman throws an opponent during a judo match. Besides throwing techniques using the hands, hips, and feet, judo includes grappling moves for pinning opponents and choke holds and leg-lock techniques. **Amwell/ The Image Bank/Getty Images**

Techniques are generally intended to turn the force of an opponent into an advantage rather than oppose it directly. A ritual of courtesy promotes an attitude of calm readiness and confidence. White belts are worn by beginners and black belts by masters. Grades in between are denoted by other colors.

Kano Jigoro (1860–1938) gained the knowledge of the old jujitsu schools of the Japanese samurai. Kano eliminated the most dangerous techniques and stressed the practice of *randori* (meaning "free practice"). But he also preserved the traditional techniques of jujitsu in the *kata* (meaning "forms") of judo. By the 1960s judo associations had been established in most countries.

Men's judo competitions were first included at the 1964 Summer Olympic Games in Tokyo and held regularly since 1972. World judo championships for women began in 1980, and women's Olympic competition began in 1992.

Judo's direction has changed since its inception. Kano designed judo to be a safe, supportive method of physical education in which opponents even helped each other to the ground. As judo competitions became more popular, however, participants began to show the competitive spirit more usually

found in Western wrestlers. They viewed judo as a sport rather than a drill or way of life. The addition of judo in the Olympic Games heightened the competitive nature of its athletes.

SUMO

Sumo is a style of Japanese wrestling in which weight, size, and strength are of the greatest importance. Speed and quickness in attacking are also useful. The object is to knock the opponent out of a ring about 15 feet (4.6 meters) in diameter. One can also achieve victory by forcing a foe to touch the ground with any part of his body other than the soles of the feet.

Between the 8th and 12th century in Japan, sumo matches were generally attended by the royal class. During that time, it was transformed from a brutal sport into one in which victory was achieved by forcing the opponent out of a circle.

Professional sumo wrestling in Japan dates from the revival of public matches after 1600 and is often called the Japanese national sport. Six great championships are held annually. They attract huge crowds.

Sumo wrestler Yokozuna Miyabiyama (right) pushes Asashoryu from the ring during a match in Ryogoku's Kokugikan Sumo Stadium, in Tokyo. **Will Robb/Lonely Planet Images/Getty Images**

Several hundred athletes make their living at this sport. A complex system of ranking leads to the designation of *Yokozuna*, or "grand champion." In Japan, only men can compete professionally in sumo wrestling.

Specially selected youths are groomed for the profession and fed a protein diet, which creates immense, bulky bodies. Agile men

weighing 300 pounds (136 kilograms) or more are common in this sport. Lengthy rituals and elaborate stances are featured in usually brief bouts that often last only a few seconds.

KARATE

Literally meaning "the art of empty hands," karate is an unarmed martial-arts discipline. It employs kicking, striking, and defensive blocking with arms and legs. It emphasizes focusing as much of the body's power as possible on the point and moment of impact.

Striking surfaces in karate include the knuckles, outer edge of the hands, ball of the foot, heel, forearm, knee, and elbow. All are toughened by practice blows against padded surfaces or wood. Pine boards up to several inches in thickness can be broken by the bare hand or foot of an expert.

In training, blows and kicks are preferably stopped within an inch of contact. Sporting matches last about three minutes before a decision is reached by judges if neither fighter has scored a clean "killing" point.

Contests of form (in Japanese, called *kata*) are also held. They feature rivals performing a set series of movements that attack and defend against those of several foes. Performances are scored by a panel of judges, as in gymnastics.

Karate evolved in East Asia over a period of centuries. It gained structure in 17th-century Okinawa, probably by people who were forbidden to carry weapons. Its world-wide popularity came about after World War II (1939–1945), when U.S. soldiers who were stationed in Japan discovered it.

Like other Asian martial-arts disciplines, karate stresses mental attitude and rituals of courtesy. It also features a complex ranking system denoted by color of belt.

Kendo

Kendo (meaning "way of the sword") is the traditional Japanese style of fencing with a two-handed wooden sword. It is descended from the fighting methods of the ancient samurai.

After military leaders unified Japan around 1600, most opportunities for sword combat were eliminated. The result was that the samurai turned swordsmanship into a means of developing discipline, patience, and skill for building character. In the 18th century, swords made of bamboo were

introduced to allow realistic fencing without risk of injury.

Kendo matches take place in a square area that measures about 30 to 36 feet (9 to 11 meters) per side. The *shinai*, or sword, varies from 43 to 46 inches (110 to 118 centimeters) in length and is made of four lengths of seasoned bamboo bound by waxed cord. All blows use the "cutting" edge of the sword, which is not

Two kendo practitioners, who are called kendoka, *prepare to strike with their bamboo* shinai. Kendoka *wear facemasks and chest protectors.* **Christian Kaden, Satori-Nihon.de/Moment Open/Getty Images**

sharp. It is usually held with both hands. Points are awarded for blows delivered upon various parts of the body.

MARTIAL ARTS IN KOREA

Korea, like China and Japan, developed fighting techniques thousands of years ago. In the 600s the Korean kingdom of Silla required that the finest young men be trained in *hwarangdo* (meaning "the way of flowering manhood"). They learned hand-to-hand and sword combat, archery, and horsemanship in becoming an elite fighting group.

Korean fighting styles struggled to survive through long periods of occupation by the Chinese and Japanese. But a true national martial art emerged after Korea gained its independence following World War II. This new style, known for its high kicks, was named tae kwon do (or "art of kicking and punching") in 1955. It was developed greatly by the South Korean general Choi Hong Hi, who drew techniques from both karate and the ancient Korean martial art of *tae kyon*.

CHAPTER 2

THE RISE OF MARTIAL ARTS GLOBALLY

Although the best known of the martial arts have come from China, Japan, and Korea, several styles were developed in other countries, including Thailand, France, and Brazil.

In addition, martial arts in general have been embraced by people in countries all over the world in the last half-century. A number of factors led to the growing popularity of martial arts in Europe and North America. The seeds were planted by American soldiers stationed in Japan after World War II in the 1940s and Korea during the Korean War of the early 1950s. The American media, particularly television and movies, also played a huge role in popularizing martial arts in the 1970s and beyond.

THAILAND AND MUAY THAI

The martial arts developed in China, Japan, and Korea were not the only ones that date back centuries. Another is muay Thai, which has its roots in Thailand.

Muay Thai is a form of boxing that features kicking, punching, kneeing, and elbowing. Little is known about its early history aside from its use as a close-combat skill in battle. One theory is that it developed after Thai people moved south from China. Others claim it had already been

Muay Thai boxers fight in a match in Lumphini Stadium in Bangkok. Muay Thai is sometimes called the art of eight limbs because fighters use their feet, shins, elbows, and hands during combat. Ingolf Pompe/LOOK/ **Getty Images**

utilized by Thai natives in defending their land from invaders.

What is certain is that muay Thai has been a staple of Thai culture for centuries. It emerged as a sport in the late 16th century. But it was also taught to soldiers and even King Naresuan (1555–1605). Even more taken with the sport in the next century was Prachoa Sua (known as "The Tiger King"). He fought in disguise in village contests and beat local champions. Interest in muay Thai exploded during his time in power. The sport again increased in popularity during the reigns of King Rama V and King Rama VI in the late 1800s and early 1900s.

The standard ring surrounded by ropes and time keeping by a clock came into use in the early 20th century. Muay Thai became codified in the 1930s as the rules and regulations of today were introduced. Television broadcasts of the sport remain an attraction as people from villages gather around to watch muay Thai matches involving their favorite athletes. By the 1990s, muay Thai bouts were attracting fighters from around the world.

EUROPE AND MARTIAL ARTS

The focus of recent research on the history of martial arts in Europe has been on the various swords and other weaponry used in combat and fencing during the Middle Ages and the Renaissance periods of European history. Most scholars agree that the close-combat use of such arms falls into the category of martial arts. The science of self-defense also became a common recreational activity in Europe.

At the Battle of Agincourt (1415), during the Hundred Years' War, English forces wielding longbows and swords defeated the French. Heavily armored soldiers during the Middle Ages and the Renaissance used swords in fencing and close combat. **The Bridgeman Art Library/Getty Images**

The masters of fencing beginning in the 12th century were not only experts in swordsmanship. They were also advanced in fighting systems of both armored and unarmored combat. The media has portrayed the knights of medieval Europe as slow and plodding in heavy armor. In reality, they were highly skilled and quick, whether wrestling or using weapons such as daggers, staffs, axes, or swords.

The advent of firearms during the Renaissance eliminated the use of martial arts skills on the battlefield. But martial arts grew as a sport. A boom of civilian schools taught students how to defend themselves. Fencing also maintained its popularity among scholars, the upper class, and royalty.

FRANCE AND SAVATE

A French martial art form known as savate and featuring both kicking and punching was created and advanced in the early 19th century by Charles Lecour. It is similar to the Thai kickboxing sport of muay Thai.

The word *savate* was used during that time to describe all forms of fighting that permitted the use of feet. Blows were delivered by the back heel to the stomach or both feet from a handstand position.

A savate match is depicted on the front page of a French newspaper in 1899. Savate allowed fighters to kick and punch. Leemage/Universal Images Group/Getty Images

Lecour opened a school in Paris to teach savate, which was also known as French boxing. Public exhibitions were held, but enthusiasm for the sport faded greatly by the 20th century.

BRAZIL AND CAPOEIRA

Among the most unusual and colorful martial arts worldwide is capoeira, the dancelike martial art of Brazil that is performed to the accompaniment of singing and music. It is a sport that requires tremendous athleticism. Participants swing their legs high in attack and somersault through the air—historically sometimes with blades strapped to their ankles or held between their toes.

Attributes such as flexibility, stamina, and quickness are far more important in capoeira than strength. Although marked by the use of graceful, fluid, and often acrobatic movements as a means to escape rather than block an attack, the "game" of capoeira, as it is called by its practitioners, can nonetheless be lethal when contact is actually made with a well-timed, well-placed blow.

In current practice, two opponents face each other within the *roda*—a circle of *capoeiristas* (practitioners of

36

On a beach in Salvador, Brazil, men perform capoeira accompanied by tambourines. Capoeira has its origins in African traditions and combines music, dance, singing, and martial arts. **Christopher Pilitz/The Image Bank/Getty Images**

capoeira)—emulating in a stylized manner the strikes and parries of combat. Music is integral to the practice of capoeira. Blows are timed to the rhythms of such

Mixed Martial Arts

Mixed martial arts has its roots in the ancient Greek sport of *pankration*, which is translated into English as "all powers." This brutal contest combined wrestling, boxing, and street fighting. The sport was performed in a small ring at the Olympic Games as early as the 7th century BCE.

The rules outlawed only biting and eye gouging. Everything else was fair game, including punching, choking, and strikes to the groin. Matches ended only when a competitor was knocked unconscious or simply gave up. Pankration was the most popular sport in the Olympics of that era. Greek ruler Alexander the Great (356–323 BCE) sought out pankration experts as soldiers.

The banning of the Olympic Games and pagan practices by Theodosius I (347–395), the Roman emperor of the East and West, in 393 CE spelled the end of pankration as a popular sport. Mixed martial arts remained dormant until it experienced a revival in the Brazilian city of Rio de Janeiro around 1925. It was popularized by brothers Carlos Gracie (1902–1994) and Hélio Gracie (1913–2009), whose father was a powerful Rio politician that had learned the craft from a Japanese immigrant.

The siblings began a jujitsu school and made a splash by issuing the "Gracie Challenge" in area newspapers. It claimed that "If you want a broken arm, or rib, contact Carlos Gracie." The brothers would take on all challengers. The matches resembled those of pankration. The matches became so popular that they had to be moved to large soccer stadiums to accommodate the throngs.

Helio's oldest son, Rorion, came to the United States in the early 1980s to promote what had become known as Brazilian jujitsu. He sought to find an organization that would back him financially. Soon the Ultimate Fighting Championship (UFC) was born. The first cable television pay-per-view event in 1993 attracted 86,000 viewers. That number had increased to 300,000 by the third event. *(continued on the next page)*

Ricardo Lamas (right) kicks Jose Aldo during a UFC featherweight bout. Featherweights weigh 136 to 145 pounds (62 to 66 kilograms). **Carlos M. Saavedra/Sports Illustrated/ Getty Images**

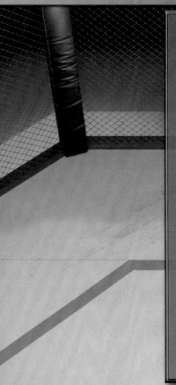

(continued from the previous page)

The UFC marketed its product as a bloody, no-holds-barred sport in which anything could happen. Its brutality raised the ire of politicians such as U.S. Senator John McCain, who sought to have the sport banned. Many states abolished it. New UFC management created rules to make the sport less dangerous. It returned to pay-per-view in 2001 with weight classes, rounds, time limits, and a list of fouls in the ring.

The revamped UFC no longer featured brawlers. It required its fighters to be more skilled as boxers, wrestlers, and mixed martial arts experts. They were forced to train extensively and remain in peak condition to perform well.

instruments as drums, tambourines, bells, and bamboo tubes, all of which accompany call-and-response songs.

The basic elements of capoeira came to Brazil from slaves of west and west-central Africa and were maintained after slavery was abolished in Brazil in 1888. The perceived physical and spiritual power of capoeira motivated the government to

outlaw the practice in the 19th century, but it was legalized in the early 20th century.

Schools teaching precise capoeira skills and strategies gained popularity in the 1930s. By the late 20th century the sport had gained an international following. Today it is practiced in clubs throughout the world by both male and female participants.

ISRAEL AND KRAV MAGA

The self-defense system of Krav Maga (which means "contact combat") was developed by Czechoslovakian Jew Imi Lichtenfeld in the late 1930s to combat widespread anti-Semitism in his community of Bratislava. It requires speed, economy of motion, and force strong enough to overwhelm an attacker.

Krav Maga is designed to strike a foe where most vulnerable. It often features blows to the groin, throat, or kidneys, as well as pokes to the eyes, head butts, or bites to the neck. Its strategies revolve around the concept of *retzef*, the Hebrew word meaning "continuous motion." Such unconventional attacking precludes it from use as a sport.

Krav Maga instructors teach defenses against knives and guns because real-world street fighting involves such weapons. Krav Maga tactics do not rely on size or strength but rather explosiveness and speed of attack. **Miguel Medina/AFP/Getty Images**

The martial art is a vital part of training for the Israeli defense and security forces. Its intended benefit is survival in any situation.

MARTIAL ARTS IN THE UNITED STATES AND CANADA

Western exposure to East Asian martial arts grew after American soldiers who had

gained knowledge of them returned home from World War II and the Korean War. But it was not until martial arts experts such as Bruce Lee and Jackie Chan gained popularity in Hollywood that the practice surged in the United States and Canada. More recent stars such as Jet Li have continued to promote martial arts in both countries. Since the 1970s, thousands of schools teaching a wide range of East Asian martial arts have thrived in North America.

The media played the biggest role in the surge of martial arts popularity in Western culture. The stars of the past have paved the way for the stars of the present and future.

CHAPTER 3

LEGENDARY MARTIAL ARTS FIGHTERS

The legends of ancient martial arts forms made their marks in East Asia, as have most that have followed. But the explosion of its popularity in Western countries, largely because of television and movies, led to others earning that distinction.

The following are considered among the greatest and most influential martial arts practitioners ever.

AKEBONO TARO

Akebono Taro was a Hawaiian-born Japanese sumo wrestler. In 1993, he became the first non-Japanese person to earn grand champion status, the highest rank in professional sumo.

Akebono learned the trade from fellow Hawaiian Jess Kuhaulua, who had become a champion in Japan. Akebono showed great strength, but struggled to maintain his balance because of his towering height of 6 feet 8 inches (204 centimeters) and enormous weight of roughly 500 pounds (about 225 kilograms). He eventually developed the skills that earned him his first tournament title in 1992.

He continued to rise through the ranks despite injuries. By the time he retired in 2001, he had won 11 championships and 566 total victories in the sumo ring. Akebono later became a respected sumo coach. He also participated in professional kickboxing and mixed martial arts competitions.

JACKIE CHAN

Jackie Chan was born on April 7, 1954. He gained fame as a stuntman, actor, and director. He performed dangerous, acrobatic stunts in films. His engaging physical humor made him an action-film star in Asia. It also helped make him popular in American cinema.

Chan spent most of his childhood in Hong Kong. His talent as a youth in acrobatics and martial arts landed him bit movie roles as a child actor and later as a stuntman. Those skills and his on-screen humor made him a success as an actor. He later showed his talent as a director in Hong Kong.

A series of action-drama films brought him fame and fortune in the United States in the 1990s and beyond. Included were *Rush Hour* (1998) and *Shanghai Noon* (2000).

Chan also founded the Jackie Chan Charitable Organization in 1988, which offered scholarships to Hong Kong youths. In addition, he worked as a goodwill ambassador for UNICEF. In 1995, Chan was presented with

Jackie Chan performs an airborne maneuver in Shanghai Noon *(2000), a film that combines adventure, action, and comedy and is set in the American West.* **Karine Weinberger/Gamma-Rapho/Getty Images**

the Lifetime Achievement Award at the MTV Movie Awards. In 2004, he created the Dragon's Heart Foundation to aid children in need in isolated regions of China. Chan also advocates conservation, animal rights, and disaster relief. In 2010, he raised more than $36 million for people around the world who were in need.

Dong Hai Chuan

Dong Hai Chuan is widely recognized as the founder of the martial art form of baguazhang. Dong grew up in a poor family in early 19th-century China. He was penniless and troubled through his childhood. Where and from whom he was taught the Taoist training methods remains unclear. But he combined those teachings with the martial arts he learned in villages during his travels as he sought work. The result was his creation of *baguazhang*, to which he later devoted his life. It gained popularity in Beijing and nearby areas.

Baguazhang is an internal martial art that features what is known as "turning the circle" as its method of stance and movement. Practitioners walk around the edge of a circle in a variety of stances while facing the center and occasionally change their direction.

Dong remained poor all his life. He died in 1882. But he became a legend through his work with such notable students as Yin Fu, Ma Gui, and Cheng Ting Hua.

BRUCE LEE

Graceful and skilled Bruce Lee brought martial arts movies to mainstream cinema in the 1970s, just as many Americans were gaining interest in Eastern culture. He died unexpectedly at age 32, which turned him into a mysterious legend.

He was born in 1940—the Chinese year of the dragon—in San Francisco, Calif. After his father—an opera singer and part-time actor—finished performing in the United States, the family returned home to Hong Kong.

Lee often visited movie sets where his father was working and soon became a child actor. He also became involved in gangs and learned kung fu to protect himself. Proving to be a quick learner of the wing chun method of defense, Lee began creating his own moves. His mother soon sent him to live with friends in Seattle, Washington, to get him away from street fighting.

Lee eventually moved to California, where he prepared actors for films involving the martial arts. He also operated schools devoted to his own technique known as *jeet kune do*—a blend of ancient kung fu and philosophy.

Lee became known to U.S. audiences with his role as the sidekick Kato in the television series *The Green Hornet* (1966–67). In the 1969 film *Marlowe*, he received notice

During the filming of Enter the Dragon *(1973) in Hong Kong, Bruce Lee performs a kung fu move. The film was the last one made by Lee before his death; many movie critics consider it to be one the greatest martial arts films ever produced.* **Michael Ochs Archives/Moviepix/Getty Images**

for a scene in which he destroyed an entire office through kickboxing and karate moves.

Troubled by his inability to find other suitable roles, however, he moved back to Hong Kong. It was there he starred in two films that broke box-office records throughout Asia and found success in the United States as *Fists of Fury* (1971) and *The Chinese Connection* (1972). Lee founded Concord Pictures and worked behind and in front of the camera for the films *Return of the Dragon* (1972) and *Enter the Dragon* (1973).

While working on *Game of Death*, Lee abruptly died on July 20, 1973. The mysterious circumstances of his death were a source of speculation for fans and historians, but the cause of death was officially listed as swelling of the brain caused by an allergic reaction to a headache medication. Documentaries such as *Curse of the Dragon* (1993) discussed his short but powerful life.

JET LI

Jet Li, whose original name was Li Lianjie, was born on April 26, 1963, in Beijing, China. He is a film actor noted for his superlative martial arts skills and his portrayals of virtuous, humble heroes.

At the age of nine, he received an award at a martial arts competition. In 1974 he won the first of five men's national championships. He retired from the sport in 1979.

In 1982 Li made his film debut in *Shaolin Si* (*The Shaolin Temple*) as a young man who learns martial arts from the monks at the revered birthplace of Chinese martial arts. *Shaolin Si* was an enormous hit and was credited with reviving interest in the martial arts in China. His name was soon changed to Jet Li, which made it easier to pronounce in other countries.

This began Li's long career as an actor, director, and producer. Though he is considered a legend, he continued to be one of the most esteemed martial arts stars well past the turn of the 21st century.

MIYAMOTO MUSASHI

Miyamoto Musashi (1584–1645), usually

A man tries to get a better look at Miyamoto Musashi. Library of Congress, Washington, D.C.

A bronze statue of Yue Fei in the city of Hangzhou, China, honors the great general and national hero. **TAO Images Limited/Getty Images**

referred to as Musashi, was a legendary swordsman in Japan. He once wrote that he had engaged in 60 duels without defeat, including some against those representing the renowned Yoshioka School of swordsmanship.

He claimed in a biography to have defeated his first opponent at age 13. He was noted to have been particularly skilled wielding two swords at once. His most famous duel was a defeat of famed swordsman Sasaki Kojiro in 1612.

Musashi was considered a frightening figure. It has been claimed that he rarely bathed or changed clothes and that he was plagued with a disfiguring skin condition. It has also been said that he cut off many a head while defending Osaka Castle in 1614 and 1615 and that his sword wizardry helped quell the Shimabara Rebellion of 1637–1638.

In 1645, Musashi completed a legendary book about swordsmanship titled *The Book of Five Rings*. He died that same year. He was later immortalized in a 1935 novel by the Japanese author Eiji Yoshikawa simply titled *Musashi*.

YUE FEI

Yue Fei was a celebrated general in China during the first half of the 12th century. He was known for his compassion in helping

the families of soldiers who had been killed in battle.

Yue boasted tremendous strength and speed, qualities noticed by martial arts instructor Zhou Tong, who had learned his craft at the legendary Shaolin Monastery. Yue mastered a complete fighting system that featured barehanded combat, weapons, and military tactics.

According to legend, Yue spread his knowledge of the martial arts form that became known as *xingyiquan*, of which he is considered by many to be its founder.

ZHANG SANFENG

Zhang Sanfeng was a Chinese priest who made his mark in the 13th century. He has been credited with originating the martial art form of tai chi chuan around 1270.

Zhang embraced the Tao religion. He lived simply in a straw hut, wore little protection in the coldest of weather, and was observed going months without food. He learned martial arts in his youth from a Taoist priest. He embraced his teachings, which included a disapproval of wealth and fame. He spent much of his life living in the various mountain ranges of China.

Tai chi boxing incorporates soft movements, including those that imitate animals
such as cats, birds, snakes, and monkeys.
Zhang's belief in and promotion of the
soothing mental effects of such movements
have motivated some to pronounce him as
the founder of internal martial arts.

Legend has it that Zhang lived 200
years, but both his birth and death dates
are unclear.

CHAPTER 4

CONTEMPORARY STARS OF MARTIAL ARTS

The modern stars of mixed martial arts generally perform for the Ultimate Fighting Championship (UFC). They receive extensive exposure on television and in live performances. They have received training in traditional martial arts, as well as boxing and wrestling.

The changes made by the UFC in the 1990s that brought about weight classes resulted in the emergence of a great number of titles and individual male and female standouts. Among them are those listed below.

RANDY COUTURE

The popularity and respect earned by Randy Couture was evident when he was honored

In Las Vegas, Nev., Randy Couture (right) fights Brock Lesnar in the UFC 91 heavyweight championship bout in 2008. Couture was inducted into the UFC Hall of Fame in 2006. Greg Choat/Sports Illustrated/ Getty Images

with the Most Valuable Fighter Award by the *Wrestling Observer Newsletter* in 2007. He was a three-time UFC champion and won titles in two separate weight classes.

Couture was born in Everett, Wash., in 1963 and grew up with the ambition of becoming an Olympic skier. He decided instead to pursue wrestling after exhibiting tremendous talent in that sport in college. He boasted an impressive background in freestyle and

Greco-Roman wrestling. Freestyle wrestling features the ability to use legs as both an offensive and defensive weapon while those techniques are prohibited in Greco-Roman wrestling. In addition, Greco-Roman wrestlers are not allowed to grab opponents below the waist or use their legs to take them down, which makes takedowns far more difficult.

Couture was a three-time National Collegiate Athletic Association (NCAA) All-American at Oklahoma State University and a five-time winner of the national Greco-Roman Championships. His wide-ranging skills in wrestling, boxing, and jujitsu made him a perfect fit for the UFC. Couture won the heavyweight belt before dropping down a class and dominating the UFC light heavyweight division in capturing that crown. He continued to fight and win titles at an advanced age. He became the oldest UFC fighter at age 43 ever to hold a crown.

RASHAD EVANS

Born in Niagara Falls, N.Y., in 1979, Rashad Evans began to gain the knowledge needed to win UFC matches as an amateur wrestler. He was a junior college national champion and All-American for Niagara Community College.

Rashad Evans (right) kicks Jon Jones in the UFC 145 light heavyweight championship bout in 2012. Evans's favorite moves are a left hook and a grappling technique called the Kimura lock. **Carlos M. Saavedra/ Sports Illustrated/Getty Images**

He has since used his lethal left hook to win the UFC light heavyweight division title. He remained unbeaten well after defeating Forrest Griffin for that crown. His victory over star Chuck Liddell was deemed 2008 Knockout of the Year by many media outlets.

Evans, who earned a degree in psychology from Michigan State University in East Lansing, first fought in the heavyweight division of *The Ultimate Fighter 2*—the second season of the mixed martial arts TV reality series *The Ultimate Fighter*. He captured that championship as well.

QUINTON RAMONE "RAMPAGE" JACKSON

Though Quinton Jackson was born in 1978 in Memphis, Tennessee, and grew up there, his

Quinton "Rampage" Jackson (left) fights Marvin "The Beastman" Eastman during the UFC 67 light heavyweight bout in 2007. This match was Jackson's debut with the UFC; he went on to defeat Eastman with a knockout punch. **Gabriel Bouys/AFP/Getty Images**

greatness in mixed martial arts became established in the PRIDE Fighting Championships in Japan. He placed second in the middleweight division of its PRIDE Final Conflict in 2003.

Jackson thrived as an all-state wrestler in high school. He originally contemplated a career in professional wrestling before deciding on MMA. Jackson recorded a mark of 11–1 in smaller venues before joining the light heavyweight division of the UFC.

Jackson eventually won a UFC title. He posted a record of 24–3–1 in his first 28 matches while gaining a reputation for his unique style inside and outside the cage. He wears a large chain-link necklace and howls like a wolf as he approaches the cage for a match. Jackson has called his howl a werewolf battle cry.

Jackson earned the Rampage nickname based on a namesake 1980s video game featuring a gorilla pummeling his way through the streets of cities. It was perceived that he destroyed opponents with a similar style. He was named "Most Outstanding Fighter" in 2007 and "Fighter of the Year" in 2008 by *Wrestling Observer Newsletter*.

B. J. PENN

Jay Dee "B. J." Penn was born in Hilo, Hawaii, in 1978. His father is of Irish ancestry. His

B. J. Penn (left) punches Frankie Edgar during the UFC 112 lightweight fight in Abu Dhabi. MMA fans admire Penn for his counter jab. Karim Sahib/AFP/Getty Images

mother has a Korean background. Because he is the youngest of his brothers, all of whom are named Jay Dee, he was called Baby Jay. He is a champion of Brazilian jujitsu. In addition, he has won two titles with the UFC.

Penn learned jujitsu as a teenager. His love of that martial art motivated a move to Northern California, where he trained under legend Ralph Gracie and rose up the belt rankings. In 2000, he became the first non-Brazilian to take first place in the black-belt division of the world jujitsu championships in Rio de Janeiro. His talent and youth earned him the nickname of "The Prodigy."

The UFC came calling in 2001. He won his first match in five minutes. He eventually won the welterweight crown in a match against Matt Hughes that lasted less than five minutes. He later won the lightweight title. Through mid-2014 he had competed in 29 UFC title fights and was only one of two UFC fighters to win championships in two separate weight classes.

Penn has also appeared in film and written a *New York Times* best-selling autobiography titled, *Why I Fight: The Belt Is Just an Accessory*.

RONDA ROUSEY

A background in judo and a desire to take an unconventional path to professional happiness led Ronda Rousey to mixed martial arts.

Rousey was born in Riverside, Calif., in 1987. She began training in the ancient

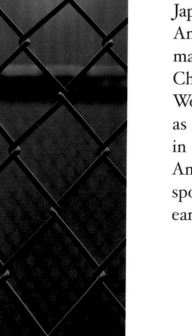

Ronda Rousey (left) won eight MMA fights with her judo move called juji gatame, *a type of cross-body arm lock. She is seen here fighting Liz Carmouche at the inaugural Women's UFC bout, which Rousey won.* **Robert Beck/Sports Illustrated/Getty Images**

Japanese art at age 11. In 1984, her mother, AnnMaria DeMars, was the first American, man or woman, to win a World Judo Championship. Ronda captured a Junior World Championship title in judo, as well as a bronze medal at the Summer Olympics in Beijing in 2008. She was also the first American woman to medal in judo since that sport became an Olympic event. She also earned a Pan Am Games crown in that sport.

The California native won her first three amateur MMA matches in less than a minute. She won her first 10 UFC matches, including eight via submission by armbar.

She quickly gained notoriety after turning pro in 2011. She was featured on the cover of *ESPN the Magazine*'s Body Issue and gained media attention in issues of *Sports Illustrated* and *Esquire* magazines.

MAURICIO RUA

A strong background in muay Thai and jujitsu transformed Mauricio Rua into a force in Ultimate Fighting Championship. He first earned the title of PRIDE Grand Champion in 2005, defeating such talent as Quinton Jackson along the way. He secured a crown in the light heavyweight division of the UFC in 2010.

Rua was born in 1981 in Curitiba, Brazil, and was motivated by his brother, Murilo Ninja, while growing up. Rua followed his brother to the Chute Boxe Academy in that country to watch him train. Encouraged by his brother, he began training for a career in mixed martial arts at the age of 16 before earning his high school and college degrees.

He established himself quickly. His defeat of Antonio Rodriguez Nogueira in a 2005 PRIDE

match is considered one of the greatest mixed martial arts matches ever. Rua then became the only fighter to score back-to-back victories over UFC Hall of Famers (Mark Coleman and Chuck Liddell). He later defeated a third Hall of Famer in Forrest Griffin.

ANDERSON SILVA

Many consider Anderson Silva the most skilled fighter in UFC. His early training included learning tae kwon do at the age of 14. The

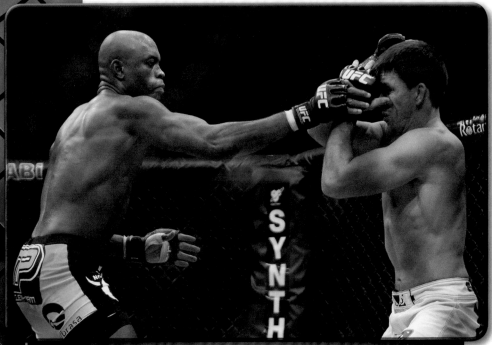

Anderson Silva (left) attacks Demian Maia during the UFC 112 middleweight bout in Abu Dhabi. Silva, who landed numerous punches and kicks, defeated Maia by unanimous decision.
Karim Sahib/AFP/Getty Images

Brazilian jiujitsu black belt and muay Thai expert has captured multiple championships, including the UFC middleweight crown.

Silva was born in 1975 in Curitiba, Brazil, and raised there. His penniless mother left him with her sister's family when he was only four years old. They could not afford to give him jujitsu lessons, so he learned the craft by watching his neighbors perform it. His family was able to afford tae kwon do lessons for him, however. He later gained greater mixed martial arts skills through capoeira before moving on to muay Thai.

He won his UFC debut in just 49 seconds, kicking off a remarkable start to his career. By the time he recorded his 22nd knockout, only four opponents had reached the second round against him.

CAIN VELASQUEZ

Cain Velasquez was born in 1982 in Salinas, Calif. Throughout his MMA career, Velasquez has been driven by his pride in his Mexican heritage. He received his work ethic from his father, who showed perseverance by walking from Mexico to the United States seven times before gaining American citizenship.

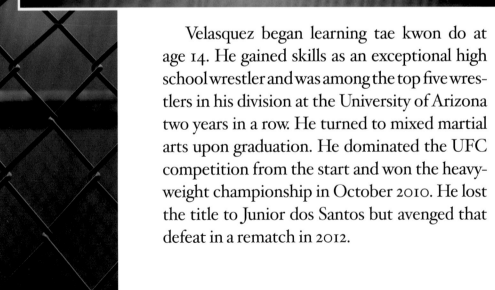

Holding a media day enables sports figures to market themselves and their organizations. Cain Velasquez (right) trains with Noad Lahat during a media day workout at American Kickboxing Academy to promote his 2013 title fight with Junior dos Santos. **Alexis Cuarezma/Getty Images**

Velasquez began learning tae kwon do at age 14. He gained skills as an exceptional high school wrestler and was among the top five wrestlers in his division at the University of Arizona two years in a row. He turned to mixed martial arts upon graduation. He dominated the UFC competition from the start and won the heavyweight championship in October 2010. He lost the title to Junior dos Santos but avenged that defeat in a rematch in 2012.

CONCLUSION

The subject of martial arts cannot be limited to one form or limited to one area of the world or one period in history.

Though martial arts originated in East Asia in ancient times, various forms exploded into use in medieval and Renaissance Europe and eventually developed in Brazil as well as North America and Western Asia.

Many regions in which martial arts were embraced featured their own unique forms, though only in China has it been linked strongly to religious and moral teachings. Yet the passion for martial arts has grown throughout the world, as evidenced by its popularity in the United States and such specific forms as Brazilian jujitsu, sumo wrestling in Japan, muay Thai in Thailand, and Krav Maga in Israel.

One cannot predict the direction martial arts will take around the world. But considering the number of forms still practiced for sport and self-defense, it seems quite certain that it will remain popular in many countries for centuries to come.

armbar A move used in martial arts as a submission hold in which the opponent's arm is locked straight out between the attacker's thighs and the elbow is hyper-extended to submission.

armored The use of equipment, such as large protective metal over clothing worn in martial arts and other fighting forms.

discipline A subject or field of study; in martial arts, a specific form such as judo or karate.

dojo A school for training in various arts of self-defense.

fencing The art or practice of attack and defense with a sword.

jujitsu The Japanese art of unarmed fighting using holds, throws, and paralyzing blows.

medieval Relating or characteristic of the Middle Ages, a period in history from about 500 CE to about 1500.

meditative Having the habit of meditating, or engaging in mental exercise (such as concentration on one's breathing or repetition of a mantra) for the purpose of reaching a heightened level of spiritual awareness.

monastery A place where a community of monks or nuns live and work.

nobility Those in the wealthiest classes of a society.

PRIDE An organization based in Japan that sponsored mixed martial arts world championship events from 1997 to 2007.

Renaissance Meaning "rebirth," the period in European history that was characterized by a surge of interest in Classical learning and values, from about the 14th century to the 17th century.

royalty Members of a royal family.

samurai A warrior serving a Japanese feudal lord and practicing a code of conduct that valued honor over life.

spiritual Relating to or consisting of spirit, not bodily or material; relating to sacred or religious matters.

submission The condition of being submissive, humble, or compliant; the act of submitting to the authority or control of another. Submission wrestling requires the opponent to vocally or visually signal defeat by his own choice.

sumo A Japanese form of wrestling in which a contestant loses if forced out of the ring or if any part of the body except the soles of the feet touches the ground.

wushu Chinese martial arts.

Canadian National Martial Arts Association (CNMAA)
1 – 3946 Quadra Street
Victoria, BC V8X 1J6
Canada
(250) 479-7686
Website: http://www.cnmaa.com
CNMAA promotes martial arts in Canada. It offers support for its members and is developing training and certification programs.

International Brazilian Jiu-Jitsu Federation (IBJJF)
USA Office
17955 Sky Park Circle, Suite C & D
Irvine, CA 92614
Website: http://ibjjf.org
IBJJF was formed by Carlos Gracie Jr. to encourage Brazilian jiu-jitsu worldwide. Its website lists events, rules (including those for referees), schools and courses, and the ranking of world athletes.

International Sumo Federation (IFS)
1-15-20 Hyakunincho
Shinjuku-ku
Tokyo 169-0073
Japan

+81-3-3360-3911
Website: http://www.ifs-sumo.org
IFS encourages interest in sumo and holds
    competitions throughout the world.

Judo Canada
212 – 1725 St. Laurent
Ottawa, ON K1G 3V4
Canada
(613) 738-1200
Website: http://www.judocanada.org
This organization is the governing body
    for judo in Canada and it supports the
    sport globally.

North American Grappling Association
    (NAGA)
36 Saner Road
Marlborough, CT 06447
(860) 295-0403
Website: http://nagafighter.com
NAGA provides news about grappling tour-
    naments and grappling rules. Its website
    posts videos of past grappling events and
    techniques of the month.

Ultimate Fighting Championship (UFC)
(702) 221-4780
Website: http://www.ufc.com

UFC was formed in 1993 to support professional mixed martial arts. Today its monthly martial arts events and championship fights are hosted around the world. The website offers resources about rules and regulations, a competition calendar, and video replays of fans' favorite fights.

U.S. Judo Federation (USJF)
P.O. Box 338
Ontario, OR 97914
(541) 889-8753
Website: http://www.usjf.com
USJF offers national standards and guidance for creating judo groups for people of all ages. On its website, it provides the USJF Judo Bulletin online.

U.S. Karate Alliance (USKA)
P.O. Box 1387
Eagle, CO 81631
(888) 979-USKA (8752)
Website: http://www.uskaratealliance.com
This organization promotes the establishment of martial art schools throughout the world. It established ranking standards, certification, and tournaments, and offers martial arts workshops.

U.S. Martial Arts Association (USMAA)
1000 Cordova Place, Suite 505
Santa Fe, NM 87505
(402) 250-4618
Website: http://wwmaa.org
Philip Porter founded this association in
1995. USMAA encourages and supports
all styles of martial arts and the highest
standards in training.

WEBSITES

Because of the changing nature of Internet
links, Rosen Publishing has developed an
online list of websites related to the subject
of this book. This site is updated regularly.
Please use this link to access the list:

http://www.rosenlinks.com/SPOR/Mart

Bradford, Chris. *Young Samurai: The Way of the Warrior*. New York, NY: Disney-Hyperion Books, 2009.

Butcher, Alex. *Judo*. Chatswood, AU: New Holland Australia Publishers, 2008.

Byers, Ann. *Krav Maga and Self-Defense: The Fighting Techniques of the Israeli Defense Forces* (MMA: Mixed Martial Arts). New York, NY: Rosen Publishing, 2013.

Dornemann, Volker, and Wolfgang Rumpf. *Taekwondo Kids: From White Belt to Yellow/Green Belt*. 2nd ed. Aachen, Germany: Meyer & Meyer Sport, 2013.

Gigliotti, Jim. *Who Was Bruce Lee?* New York, NY: Grosset and Dunlap, 2014.

Harmon, Daniel E. *Grappling and Submission Grappling* (MMA: Mixed Martial Arts). New York, NY: Rosen Publishing, 2013.

"The Immortal Zhang Sanfeng." Retrieved June 13, 2014 (http://www.pureinsight.org/node/5952).

Inman, Roy. *The Judo Handbook* (Martial Arts). New York, NY: Rosen Publishing, 2008.

Marx, Christy. *Jet Li*. New York, NY: Rosen Publishing, 2002.

Pawlett, Ray. *The Karate Handbook* (Martial Arts). New York, NY: Rosen Publishing, 2008.

Pawlett, Ray. *The Tai Kwon Do Handbook* (Martial Arts). New York, NY: Rosen Publishing, 2008.

Rielly, Robin L. *Karate for Kids*. North Clarendon, VT: Tuttle Publishing, 2004.

Ritschel, John. *The Kickboxing Handbook* (Martial Arts). New York, NY: Rosen Publishing, 2008.

Roza, Greg. *Brazilian Jiu-Jitsu* (MMA: Mixed Martial Arts). New York, NY: Rosen Publishing, 2013.

Roza, Greg. *Muay Thai Boxing* (MMA: Mixed Martial Arts). New York, NY: Rosen Publsihing, 2013.

Scandiffio, Laura. *The Martial Arts Book*. Toronto, ON: Annick Press, 2010.